MONKEY POKEY

Written by Martin Boon
Illustrated by Lauren Scott

This book is completely inspired by and dedicated to…

Gypsy Pixie

*…who has a wonderful and imaginative way with her
vocabulary. My love and my muse,
I'm a lucky boy xx*

Monkey Pokey

Monkey Pokey © Martin Boon 2022

First Published by Boon Boon Books 2022
ISBN 978-1-7397330-0-1

Text © Martin Boon, 2022
Illustrations © Lauren Scott, 2022

Typeset by The Book Refinery Ltd
www.thebookrefinery.com

A record of this book is available from the British Library catalogue.

Printed on paper from responsible sources.

This book belongs to...

....

Dated...

If I am unfortunate enough to lose this wonderful book & you've found it, I hope you enjoy it as much as I did.

chapter one
Monkey Pokey

Monkey Pokey awoke and sat up in his tree
"Why are all the other monkeys looking at me?"
He rubbed his eyes in case he was still dreaming
No, he was right, one hundred bright monkey eyes beaming

He asked the nearest, "What's the fascination with me?
Have I parked my butt in an inappropriate tree?"
He just raised his furry finger as if to say hush
Then with his primary digit did give Pokey a push

Pokey jumped back with much surprise and confusion
Then all the monkeys came to the same conclusion
One hundred index digits raised and ready he could see
"It seemed all the monkeys want to be pokeying me"

He decided it best he should leave the woody retreat
So took to flight, but as he jumped up, slipped on his feet
Always the quickest way to get down from being high
If only he had taken lessons and learnt how to fly

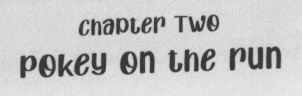

chapter Two
Pokey on the run

Crunchy sounded Pokey as he hit the leafy ground
From the breaking of bones there wasn't a sound
He shook himself to try to wake up from the bump
Slowly checked himself, and found on his head a lump

He noticed the bright monkey eyes looking from on high
Wondering what else the monkeys up there could spy
Pokey decide to get up and make himself scarce
As the eyes of the monkeys started to look fierce

Pokey took a moment to slowly climb to his feet
Then making haste down the fruity lined street
Not being a runner, he started to pant and sweat
He wondered after running how hot he would get

A clearing appeared in front of Pokey's sweaty face
A tree walled oasis with cool refreshing water in place
Remembering that if it's got teeth it ain't a banana
Last time he was careless, he got bit by a piranha

Chapter Three
Monkey Meets Rhinoceros

Pokey looked around and moved now with much caution
Remembering how the fish from his rear removed a portion
He got to the water's edge relatively safe and sound
Then caught sight of a creature within, huge and round

The creature lurched out of the lake, from under
It reared up as if scared and then screamed like thunder
Pokey fell back in surprise, this creature looked dangerous
As he scrambled back, he recognised the uppity rhinoceros

Pokey ceased his retreat and slowly stood up erected
It seemed it was animosity from the creature he detected
The Rhino's huge horn drew Pokey's closest attention
He wondered if his monkey problem should get a mention

Our hero stood tall with questions ready to broadcast
But soon changed his mind and started to run fast
Away from the Rhino, so fast the trees got blurry
Until a sudden stop, as he hit a wall, orange and furry

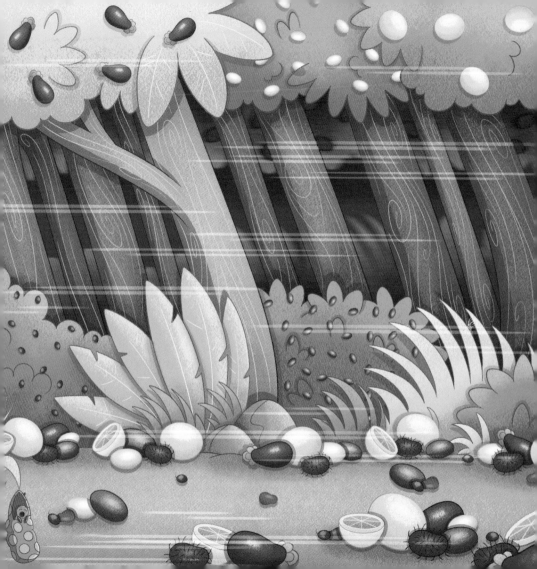

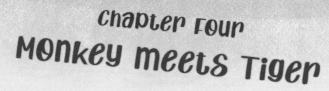

Chapter Four
Monkey meets Tiger

The Tiger seemed to not want Pokey for tea
So he moved close so it could hear his plea
After Pokey's request, he seemed most unbothered
Then licked his lips and in hunger he hovered

At this point Pokey had such a strange feeling
That soon for a meal Tiger would find him appealing
So he smiled and bowed and slowly backed away
Didn't want to be on the menu this particular day

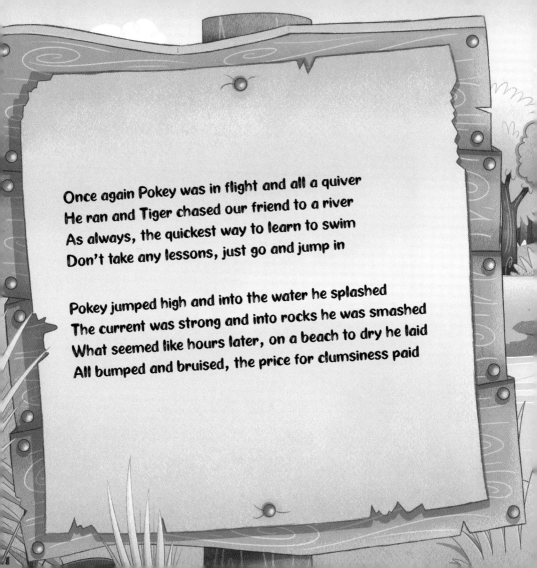

Once again Pokey was in flight and all a quiver
He ran and Tiger chased our friend to a river
As always, the quickest way to learn to swim
Don't take any lessons, just go and jump in

Pokey jumped high and into the water he splashed
The current was strong and into rocks he was smashed
What seemed like hours later, on a beach to dry he laid
All bumped and bruised, the price for clumsiness paid

Chapter Five
Monkey Meets Cobra

Pokey lay there, drying on the edge of the lake
Something moved and hissed, Pokey found a snake
The Cobra raised itself up, flared its neck, hissed more
Pokey had found the worst trouble, fell right at its door

The snake looked agitated and struggling to calm
Looking to the river as if there was pending harm
Pokey looked at the river and then the other side
There in the grass he saw baby snakes trying to hide

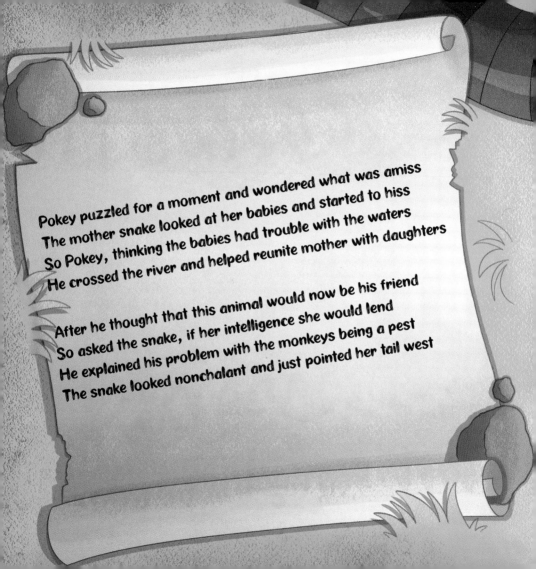

Pokey puzzled for a moment and wondered what was amiss
The mother snake looked at her babies and started to hiss
So Pokey, thinking the babies had trouble with the waters
He crossed the river and helped reunite mother with daughters

After he thought that this animal would now be his friend
So asked the snake, if her intelligence she would lend
He explained his problem with the monkeys being a pest
The snake looked nonchalant and just pointed her tail west

Chapter Six
Pokey Meets People

Pokey reached the edge of the forest and into a large clearing
A fence and houses he could see, the sound of voices cheering
Pokey ran to the gap in the fence, to see what the noises mean
Bald monkeys all in a group, one turned and Pokey had seen

Pokey looked up at the kindly face of the monkey with no hair
He asked the question about why other monkeys treated him unfair
"What do you mean "All the other monkeys were Pokeying me?""
"Well I'm a Monkey Pokey," He said, "Look, I'm sure you can see"

The man looked down at Pokey and started to giggle
It's not what's outside that counts, it's what's in the middle
He took a cloth from his pocket, and started to clean
"You're not a Monkey Pokey, but People Pokey I mean"

The man picked up Pokey, the crowd was soon past
In through a door way, through rooms til the last
He pointed to the mirror and asked Pokey what could he see
Pokey looked and said, "There's a boy smiling back at me."

The End

A huge thanks to all the people that have helped
make this book possible…

Mrs CJ 'Gypsy Pixie' Boon, Miss K Mcloughlin,
Miss L Scott, Mrs C Parks, Mr M Carson, Mr AG Boon,
Mrs G Boon, Mr C Boon and Mr J Boon.

Also, the interest, encouragement and enthusiasm of all
the above plus Mr L Robertson, Mr J Hall,
Mr M Southall, all the staff of Buxtons (Penkridge),
especially Sophie, staff and children of the Saffron
Walden County High School, namely Miss J Lister,
Abigail, Erin, Holly and Joanna.

Thank you all.

An epic voyage of discovery

Critics are saying,

"Wow, that ending blew my mind." - ★★★★★ M Carson

"I'm impressed, great work. Excellent." - ★★★★★ J Hall